Rush
Of
Many
Waters

Also by Pauly Hart

Rush of Many Waters:

Volume Fifteen

By Pauly Hart

Contents

Shorts

Painting the Lazy Susan

Part One:

1

Perhaps the only real regret that Saffron had was pulling the trigger a little too hard. When the .22 came out of the barrel, it pulled slightly to the left, missing Edgar's eye. Edgar grimaced, dropped to his knees and let out a cry of pain. His gun clattered to the basalt beside him, like dead man's bones. It was now or never. She leapt up and sprinted over to where his rifle lay, doing a somersault and picking it up with the roll. Dodging away and to the right, she kept running.

"I'm going to rip out your spleen and tie it on my hat!" He cried.

"That's oddly specific!" She called back to him. "I told you not to come on our land, or there would be hell to pay!"

She had ran up behind the barn. He would only be dazed for a moment longer. Maybe she could squeeze off a shot and clip his kneecap to slow him down. She chambered a round in the Winchester Chuckster and eased out slowly to see how he lay. He wasn't there. Where the hell was he then? She scanned left, then right. Nowhere.

"You pay now, scrawny runt!" Edgar howled right behind her. In what seemed like slow motion, he bent over her and scooped her up with his enormous hand. He raised her head to his mouth and bit her head off.

2

"Well that sucks." Bryce said, putting the controllers down and taking off the headset.

"Hey," said his mom, "watch your language."

"What? Sucks? That isn't a bad word." Bryce said.

"You would if you knew what it stood for." His mom said.

Dad chimed in from the other room: "No Shit! Watch your damn mouth!"

"Dad!" Bryce said at the same time his mom said: "Henry!"

His dad laughed and was quiet again.

His mother turned to him, arms crossed. "Anyway: 'Sucks' is short for "To suck someone off' - like fellatio." His mother looked very sternly at him. "And we don't talk that sort of way around here. You never know who could be listening."

"What's fellatio?" Bryce asked, even though he was getting more and more uncomfortable.

His mother picked up a pillow and pretended to straighten the cover. "You know... S-E-X."

"Oh." Bryce turned back toward the empty screen. He didn't want to talk about that at home. Mom was right. He made a mental note not to use that word again.

The next morning Saffron was at the gate, waiting for him.

"What did you think of the app?" She said, almost offhandedly.

He knew her better than that. She was baiting him. Pretty strange for her but he decided to play along.

"Oh, it was no biggie. Too bad you got killed though." He said with a shrug.

She was interested.

"You got killed?" she asked, amazed.

"Yeah," He said. "He bit your head off.

She turned back to the gate, silent.

She stood for a long time, not saying anything.

"You really died?" She said slowly.

"Yes. The giant bit off my head."

"Wow. That sucks." She said.

"That's what I said, but then my mom told me not to say it like that, cause it means sex." he said quietly.

"No shit?" she said.

"No shit." he said.

Just then two other children arrived and they waited for the gate to click open.

Third class was solar history. The teacher was at the front of the class droning on about the early fall of Rome. It was boring stuff. Bryce kept sending Saffron notes on her pilot.

"Did he tell you he would eat your spleen?" Bryce asked.

"Yes." She replied.

"Did he tell you that he would wear it as a hat?" He asked.

"Yes." She replied, then added. "Stop it."

"What did you tell him?" He asked.

No answer.

"Did you say something funny?"

No answer.

"Did you say that it was oddly specific?"

"Yes. SHUT UP." She said out loud, turning to him.

The teacher quit the lecture, and hovered to Saffron's seat, looked her squarely in the eye.

"Was that directed at me?" the teacher asked?

Before Saffron could answer, the teacher smacked her on the backside of the head, almost knocking her out of her seat.

Bryce had waited for her after school by the bike rack. Not that there were any bikes to ride out here anyway. Their transfer station was five miles out from the residential border and no trams ran after 1600. But he skipped his gate bus for her anyway. He knew her parents wouldn't come. Even though they were at home, they would be working.

At 15 after the hour, the front door of the school opened, and she walked out. Her head was bandaged and she had been crying. He ran up the steps to her. She didn't acknowledge him. He had been hoping for something. He took her bag and put it over his shoulder. She started to protest, then looked away.

At the base of the steps, she stopped, looking up and down the tracks.

"We gotta walk huh?" she asked.

He nodded his head.

"You don't have to carry that for me." She said.

"It was my fault. I'm sorry." He hadn't meant to cry but now he felt his cheeks turning hot and his eyes watering up.

She heard it in his voice though. She turned to him and looked him in the eyes.

"It's not your fault. It's not. It's their fault. They shouldn't be allowed to do that. It's mean and cruel and stupid."

She took a step towards him and hugged him.

The school street lights began to turn off around them. She didn't care. She held him even tighter.

6

They arrived back at the neighborhood gate well after it was dark. It had been a long walk, most of time they walked in silence, not saying anything. She had avoided the subject of the reprimand by the teacher but now she decided to open up.

"I was sent to Mister Schole, at the office. He read the teacher's note about the incident and marked on my permanent record." She said. He started to object or apologize, or both, but she put her hand up. "It wasn't a demerit, so it won't affect anything… It was marked as 'Medical.'"

She smiled.

"Let's talk about it tomorrow. Can you try the game I made again tonight?" She asked.

"No. It's too late. Mom will be on the hyper until morning, and dad gets off after I go to bed." He said.

"It's alright. Just… Next time when the giant comes for you don't stay behind the barn. You have to-"

He cut her off. "Don't tell me! I want it to be a surprise!" He almost yelled.

She laughed. "Alright, alright."

He hugged her.

"I love you Saffron." He said.

She looked at him with an odd look.

"You'd better. We're supposed to be married in a couple of years." She said, took her bag, and waved goodbye to him.

This is the story of a chair. No, really it isn't. It's the story of a boy who was in love with a chair. Really. It's that kind of story. A boy in love with a chair, who didn't care what others thought of him or his infernal addiction. The chair was like many ordinary chairs. It was an indoor chair, white and wooden and cut the way that the Shakers used to cut theirs. Built for the formidable uses around the house and then hung on the wall when not in use, so as better to sweep the floors.

The boy's name was Harold. He was a young man who had grown up the way that many young men grow up in the Midwest. He had played Little League as a child, gone to church youth group and preferred Reese's Pieces over M&Ms. He had broken his tailbone in the fourth grade and this was (to many people's estimation) the beginning of his love affair with the chair.

Harold was nine years old when he broke his tailbone. No, it wasn't in baseball, as you may imagine... Rather, it was on roller skates at the Big Skate, the local skating rink. The year was 2004 and Big Skate was a little lean on the money so their shoes were not in good repair; as a matter of fact, the whole place was held up by hopes and dreams and three mortgages. The owner's name was also Harold, but that does not play into our story at all and can promptly be forgotten.

Harold had been forced to stay at home for two weeks. He couldn't walk, for if he did, he would cry. He couldn't lie in his bed, or on the couch, or even on the ground – the pain was so intense. But he could sit on a certain white chair that had sat in the mud room; only used when people put on their boots or took them off again in the snow or mud. Upon finding this out, the chair was moved into the kitchen where he did most of his recovery from his injury.

His father, a stern man by the name of Greggory, had not immediately seen Harold's use of only one chair as a repository of good-thinking and kept moving it back to the mudroom upon his arrival home from work every day. But Harold would just move it back to the kitchen, and there he would spend the rest of the day drawing cartoons until it was supper time. His mother thought it was a fine idea to have Harold so close to her during the day and had grown used to him being there with her. During these times, he and his mother would chat about life, schoolwork, and of course, comics.

One day, while Harold's mother was cutting carrots to add to a stew, she and Harold came upon the discussion of school.

"You'll be going back to school soon young man. You'd best prepare your mind for that. You'll be very behind on your school work." she said, in that motherly way, neither judgmental nor cheerful. His mother was great at that.

"Oh, I know. But I've been doing my take-home work every day and I'm going to be ok." he said.

"Well. Just because Reginald comes over with it and you do it here, that doesn't mean that you have the full discipline of being in a classroom. It's really very different when you have hands-on help from the teacher." she said.

"Yeah, I guess." he said, and sighed.

That night, his father and mother decided that he was well enough to go back to school. There wasn't really any cause for Harold to stay at home anymore and draw comics. Harold disagreed. That day when Reginald came over with the take-home work, he told Reginald the news that he was going back.

"That sucks." Reginald said. "If I were you I would never go back."

"I know!" Harold said. "But my mom and dad are making me."

"Barf-a-roni." Reginald said. Harold laughed. Reginald always said the funniest things.

The next day at school was horrible. He had to take the bus but he cried all the way there, because of his tailbone. The other kids made fun of him, even though Reginald told them all to shut up. Kids are just horrible sometimes. But then he cried in the classroom as well, and Reginald gave up defending him.

"You didn't cry when you were home." Reginald said with disgust.

That night he told his parents about his miserable day. He told them that every time he sat down it hurt, and he cried.

"Well you're not crying now." his father said.

"Because I'm sitting in my chair!" Harold whined.

The next day, the same thing happened. Harold cried so much that his teacher sent him to the school nurse and they phoned his mother. She came and got him and took him home. He cried on the way home and immediately went and sat in his chair. The pain went away and he quit crying. When his father got home, he and Harold's mother decided that they should go back to the doctor. Tomorrow was Saturday and they got in to see the doctor early in the morning. The doctor liked them and came in early. He ordered X-rays.

"See this area here?" The doctor pointed to the X-ray, when they were all in the room together. He had a little stick that looked to Harold like a magic wand. "Usually when we see a vestigial tail, it is higher and very apparent at childbirth. Most infants lose their tail in utero, but Harold here, has sprouted a little early. And that's the funny thing about this pseudo tail. It's not only coming from his coccyx, but it's separated the entire Sacra along the S1-S5 lines. It's quite amazing. Usually they are hard-fused together, but Harold's have separated, probably during his injury, and now they are forming not as a pseudo tail alone, but are giving way to growth. See here?" The doctor pointed again at the very bottom of the tailbone, "This is now coccyx plus three. We're calling it Sacrum six, seven, and eight. S6-S8. It's quite amazing, really."

"That - that looks like the groove in the back of Harold's chair." His father said.

"His chair?" The Doctor asked.

And they told him all about Harold's special chair. The Doctor was surprised about this, and asked Harold about it.

"That's the only place I can sit." Harold said. "Everything else makes me cry." He was embarrassed.

"Can't you do something?" His dad asked.

"Well. Unless we want to spend hundreds of thousands of dollars on surgeries, there's really nothing that we should do. Harold is a healthy young man." The Doctor said.

They decided to do nothing. Harold's tail grew a little longer until he hit puberty, and then stopped. It was three feet long.

And that's the story. Harrold took his chair with him wherever he went. It was an odd little sight, seeing him carry around a study wooden chair, but then again, we've seen stranger things, haven't we?

Shorts

Sky Blue

People saw him and they walked away
He cried in the park
He was alone and his dog had left him
He was wearing that make up for that special occasion
He continued to sit and finally sighed
As his left arm rest on the picnic basket
And the tears fell like rain on that old blanket
That red and white checkered blanket
That his mother had given him as a special gift
As he looked at his oversized shoes
As his makeup ran...

The sound of crushed leaves and the smell of soap
He smelt and heard and then looked
And turned his head slightly to the right and behind him
There was a blue poodle skirt and a vision of the '50s
As she held an embroidered kerchief in her right hand
That kerchief her uncle had gin her to match her skirt
The initials D.M.J. were accented in sky blue
And it matched her skirt
She cocked her head slightly to the left
Smiled, and extended the kerchief...

He had ruined that kerchief with his makeup
But she didn't mind, because she had plenty
As a matter of fact, she told him to keep it
And he did, tucking it into his right pants pocket
His oversized red with white polka-dot pants pocket
And she smiled again, and it matched his smile
Because he had just started smiling
And far away a peacock called from across the lake

And they both laughed...

because it had been a long time
since either of them had heard a peacock.

stop means stop

he held her down
pillow wet, lights off
gripping and yelling
she wanted him off
she wanted to die
anything but this
not here, not now
oh God, save me
he hits her hard
pulls off her skirt
there is no escape
stop she says
he hits her again
stop she begs
stop means stop

Fuel

Anger buried still smolders
Anger choked will explode
Anger kindled will burn
Burning into the ashes of forgiveness

Fifth Pillar
(Inspired by Sun Tzu)

A table needs but four legs.
Any less and it becomes unstable.
Add another and it is always askew.

The fifth pillar need not be strong.
Only angled and similar to the rest.
At any place under the table place it.

Now your shift begins. Now you see.
Any longer and you move balance away.
Any shorter and the illusion of reliability

It is only there to ruin. The terrible pillar.

Aslan Itch
(Reflections of C.S. Lewis)

I itch away at complacency
    until it subsides.

Scratching at apathetic views
    that I cannot quite reach.

I peel away my mediocrity
    with growing pain.

He ripped away my lack of love
    and it all fell away.

In chunks of flesh that I lie among.
With blood and scraps of cloth around.

I quiver and burn with searing pain.
The air is cold. My sinuses drain.

Plunged down in the untouched pool.
I'm born anew to the world of men.

New skin, baby and beet is that of mine.
The avenging scales of death are gone.

And now, baptized in frozen numbness,
I arise no more the dragon, but man.

On High

Within life's' sweetest melody
   And in the finest harmonies
The birds and angels sweetly sing
   You are enthroned

For in the mountains that boast gold
   And in the valleys yet untold
Upon those crags and cliffs so bold
   You are enthroned

The sweetest nectar I could taste
   The fairest maiden I'd embrace
Could never try to take the place
   Of you enthroned

For upon life's long melody
   And in lost valleys that none see
There could no sweeter nectar be
   You are enthroned

Free to decide

Fearless and free we change ourselves

to become more than we could have imagined
Our lives become a small stone
   Washed upon the shore of limitless supply
As we stand in the horizon of our fortune
   And look back on accomplishments forsaken
We mentally see our past and imagine a future
   Less provocative than we have ever seen
Full of choice and futile hope we realize
   that the choices desired are often destroyed
Fearless and free We free ourselves
   Fearless and free we heal ourselves
Let no man rule your destiny
Let no man rule your life

Some people never do

Some don't ever realize
The laughter and joy in your eyes.
Some people don't ever find the reason why
But I know that Jesus cared, for He died.
Though it seemed a struggle
Though it seemed too hard.
Jesus I know that in truth
You are my only trump card.

Those hurting and dying just don't understand
That you stretched forth your all,
when you stretched forth your hand.
With hinds feet on high places I will strive
I'll give my utmost for his highest though I die.
Sometimes all those hurdles seem way too high
I know I'm not perfect, but with Jesus I try.

Some people don't find out till it's too late.

Everyday
I get a little bit closer
To your love my God
Everyday
I feel a little bit nearer
To your love

And I see your glory
All around

My eyes and the
Bible before me
Everything
Everything

Take care of the people that pray for me
Like my mom my grandma and Olivia
I don't know why they care but they do

Take care of my friends
And my ex-wifes aborted children
May I see them in Heaven again

Take my heart
Take my hands
And do with them
What you will

Take my family
Take my brother Timmy
Take my dad too
And do with him what you will
His first name's Bill

Essays

Of Smell

I remember when I was six, there was a certain thing that I liked to do. Every time my mother would come home from the grocery store I would root through the bags looking for a new jar of Peanut Butter. More often than not there would be a new glass jar of Peter Pan Peanut Butter just waiting for me to pry it open. "Pop!" would be the sound and then the whoosh of goodness. I would take a deep whiff of that childhood wonder and then proceed to grab a knife and bread and make myself the largest and globbiest mess of a sandwich that would be my lunch and (aside from parental chastisement) my dinner as well.

Then along came pubescence and with it, the loss of smell. "Olfactory Deficiency" There were no doctors tests. There was no scientific survey. My parents were not the richest, and there was not much they could do besides pray. But pray they did. Ever since birth, I was afflicted with one thing or another, from a disease that only eighteen other people had lived from, to sway-back, to heart murmurs, to weak lungs... prayer had been the answer every time. Prayer from Happy Caldwell, Charlie Capps, Marilyn Hickey, and even a seventeen year old evangelist known as Roberts Liardon had been my blessing from the Lord. Healing after healing accompanied me on my journey in life and I indeed had been a most blessed person. But still, no smell.

Upon my arrival into College, and the embarrassment of always wearing too much cologne (a bad thing), or not wearing enough (even worse)... I proceeded to research my disorder. And though I was no scholar in the matter, I found that smell is the number one synapse response on long-term memory activation. And that taste was up to 70% smell associated. I wondered and remembered: YES, most of my memories did involve smell in some way, and YES, I couldn't hardly taste a thing. Most of my taste was based on texture and sweets. Prime Rib to me was bland and tasteless, while Tapioca Pudding was by far a much better choice in my mind. Of course, you may wonder about that, but it made perfect sense to me. But in all of the findings, I discovered one thing: There wasn't much I could do. And upon finding that, I resigned to live my life without the blessing shared by all others in the world. A blessing I figured I would never partake of again.

But why not? This question bugged me all through college and into marriage and children. Why couldn't I have all five of my senses working in their proper order. I knew in my heart that what Isaiah 53 said was true, and again in I Peter 2:24... That by HIS STRIPES we were made whole! I believed it, but I don' think that I was convinced that such a big and important God would be meek and caring enough to come and touch such a small affliction. I believed God could and would heal me, but did not BELIEVE IT FULLY. And such was my plight, that in putting my trust in Him, I had not yet put my entire trust in what He could do. So I was living in West Lafayette, Indiana and attending a happy little church where God was indeed blessing his people, and I began talking about it to the few true friends that I possessed, and even to my future wife, who I was dating at the time. Could I be healed? Yes! But if God did in fact want to heal me, then He would have one of His shepherds tell me. The first time an alter call went up for this specific thing, I would go and claim it.

Over a year passed, and I married and we moved to Tulsa Oklahoma. My wife and I had been looking for a church, for all the ones we visited seemed aloof and chilling. We were sure that all of Gods people here in this wondrous city were not all the same, and so it happened that on our first visit to Open Bible Fellowship, Pastor Joel Budd came and said hello to us and prayed this simple prayer over me: "Just get him plastered Lord... Floor him."

Well I was floored. During the Sunday night service Memorial Day weekend, Pastor Linda Budd called out for someone to be healed of nose problems. Little did she know that she was calling out into existence the prayer I had prayed in faith almost two years ago. That night I was healed. I lay on the floor, and after several minutes I began to experience what I can only describe as thrilling. I felt my upper sinus cavity 'pop' and began to realize that I was aware of a strange sensation in my head... Smell! I could smell! I first smelt the air. and then was aware of someone gently wafting an oil with a hint of incense in it, and then was aware that I had been given a peppermint. WOW! That was the best mint I had ever had! Ha! To think of all this I had been missing and now here it was... as real as ever. The carpet, my Bible, everything took on a new life, as I was able to "see" it in a different light. Those next days were really wild! I began to clean things around the house that I never knew needed cleaning. I was able to enjoy my wife's scented candles, and even sprayed some of her perfume, so I could know what it smelled like. What a blessing. All that next week and even now I go around to things and when no one is looking bend over and give it a precautionary sniff. Do I look strange? Perhaps... Do I care? Not in the slightest. I have tasted and have smelt this beautiful world the way God intended me to, and I am ever thankful for even increasing my senses. Oh yes I am healed, Praise God, But I will not be satisfied until I see Him face to face.

`believe`

there are lives that could be touched there are lines that could be extended sometimes when you wake up in the middle of the night and you hear yourself crying out to no one it seems like a much more likely event that the heart sees much more than the eyes let on and what is actually registered there in the soul of a wise man who once said that it is not best to try and do things right but that you should just do it forcefully and with no loss so don't try but just do it and that is where the Loneliness ends and where the wolves do not prowl for putrid bloody flesh but where truths become a reality for stories that are interwoven with the mesh of the anti-void when the sands of time become hard clay and the shores of existence become quicksand that is where nightmares become truth and the sand-man slips under your pillow and the gods of triumph hide their faces then we shall see who is the overcomer and who is the one who rises up out of the ashes of our charred humanity and sees the fullness of the God-head and that which is real becomes false at the end of the line like a very bad b movie with effects that are not special so is love not based on touch however love based upon principles of true humanity is seen as a threat to the integral system of all the worlds governing powers that with one fell swoop they should come down and spread their wings and fly like hungry birds hungry from winter like death by cold is the way that lives expand and shatter for a life without hope is no life at all

Cultural truth

What is the whole truth? As discussed before, the Bible declares itself as the truth. The sum of Gods words translated in perfect condition are true words indeed. The word of God is the written tradition that transcends any other tradition handed down in any culture it permeates.

Every culture has its own folklore. Its own history. The most wonderful thing in my opinion about the word of God is that it gives us guidelines for every culture on this planet Earth. The entire basis to build any culture on.

Every culture declares oral tradition as well as written to its initiates. Whether they be born into the society or be converts, defectors, or immigrants. The tradition handed down to United States citizens lies along the vein of George Washington, Daniel Boone, Abraham Lincoln, Martin Luther King Jr. and the like. But these traditional stories also hold cultural truths as well. Like the cultural truth that telling lies is wrong. (i.e. George Washington chopping down the cherry tree).

Every "ethos" as the Bible describes in the book of the book of Revelations chapter five, verse nine and again in chapter seven, verse nine; the word sets upon itself certain views of what is right and what is wrong. Here I am not referring to "laws". I am talking about morals per se. I am talking about the complete ethos of what is true and what is false.

It is not fair to say that there is just one culture of the U.S.A. There are hundreds. Perhaps thousands of justifiable culture groups represented here. So, perhaps someone deep in the neck of some wood is raised with the ideology that people of a darker color are to be treated as animals. Morally, they can engage in murdering those people without breaching his moral code, whatsoever. On the same token, there are perhaps those who have been raised with the opposite views. That those of a lighter color are naught but monsters to be taken out of their supposed power. That person can engage in a violent act of what the rest of the geo-political country would agree to be wrong. However, morally these people are not committing a crime in their own mind. Morals. If "White Supremacy" or "Black Power" is your moral mindset, then you are free to act within it.

In the U.S.A., there is the "collective moral attitude" that these two extremes are wrong. What makes them wrong? What makes us decide that THIS is wrong or THIS is right. There are two main things in this country, The first was that it was founded on the word of God, and the second is the fact that there are so many diverse cultures here... It makes it very easy to find the middle ground of morality. Now you and I know that a "good balance" is no substitution for the word of God. You and I know that to have any truth or falsehood, we must first go back to the one who gave them to us to begin with. Back to God. Not just parts of him. Not the tidbits that fit you. But the entirety of Him.

One of the chief examples of not taking the sum of Gods word as truth is the example of Apartheid. Apartheid was the practice of racial segregation in South Africa from 1951-1991. The Afrikaners (Those white south Africans of predominantly Dutch and German descent) put into slavery those of the Zulu, Swazi and other black tribes. Apartheid reigned when the Afrikaners were in power. Part of what the Afrikaners believed at that time was that all blacks were marked for their sin, as mandated by God. This is a misrepresentation of the scripture when God marks Cain for his sin against Able.

What was the belief of this culture? How did they take one verse of scripture and determine what should be done from there to so many a people? Was it the "truth" that made them "right"? What I mean by that is that "right and wrong" are here (and oftentimes elsewhere) confused with "true and false". These mix-ups have been the cause of many a Governmental error. There have been executions, beating, jailings, and many other atrocities for the incorrect perception of truth. Just because one truth is present, doesn't mean that you exclude the contexts of the truths around it. You cannot pick and choose which truths are right for you. All the truth of the word of God is truth for you. Whether you agree or must force yourself to submit. It is true nonetheless.

 The common but gross mistake is to take the Bible and fit it into your culture. What is correct is to have the culture fit into the Bible. The reliability of the Word is always there. Whenever you (or your culture as a whole) ever runs into a seemingly unsolvable predicament… you may always look to the word. On the converse, a culture that lets the Bible fit into the gaps and chinks of their cultural identity will surly crumble when stress comes. The Bible is not intended to be a patchwork to "fix-all" in your life. It was and is intended to be the very foundation of any existence… personal, as a culture, or as we have in this country, a network of cultures that make up our make-up.

Hart Energies Oil and a Billy Goat

I didn't really want to go back to the deli/coffeeshop life and wasn't interested in trying my hand at being a youth pastor again. I was in a quandary and so I did what any rational man would do, and went to work for my dad in the oil business. It was pretty good pay at $15 an hour and my jobs were highly physical but pretty lax.

I spent a lot of time in the middle of Kansas, on top of batteries looking over the flat plains, thinking and praying. At night, (with light pollution at almost a zero), I charted and studied the movements of stars, the moon, and Venus. It was a pretty great gig and I got to know my dad as an adult for the first time that I also was an adult. He's a neat guy. He also thinks I'm crazy for believing the Bible on several things. He's a geologist by trade. He studies underground rock formations to find and drill crude oil and natural gas. It's his passion and hobby and he's pretty good at it. But when we would talk about the creation event he would always fall de facto back on his limited understanding of the old earth creation account, denying the deluge (the flood of Noah) and denying anything about the Biblical shape of the earth. To him, NASA had it all figured out. "Your grand-dad didn't believe we walked on the moon. He thought they were somewhere out in Arizona," he would say and laugh.

But all was not lost. We had a great time getting to know each other, and he's become a great friend to me. At the same time I was comparing notes on Orion's Belt to the Pyramids of Giza, he was looking at shale deposits and how much oil cut mud lay in the Anadarko Basin. We each have our passion I guess. But this was the stock I was raised from, this man who wrote his master's thesis on stalactite formations... This was my dad and I could learn a lot about my sense of passion by studying him. And I did. It was excellent. God? Yes. Flat earth? Sadly, no. I never reached out to my brother or my three step-sisters or step-mother about any of this. Already the black sheep of the family, it would not have been a good thing.

Back at home, John and I moved out from the apartment we were living at and got a place to ourselves. Well, Dan was there, but he was always holed up in his room. It was at this wonderful juncture that we would create music, work day jobs and at night either watch survival shows or conspiracy documentaries. Still, no mention of the flat earth. John, like me, is an INTP personality and you can't convert those types of people to anything. We are a tough breed who never dies... No wait, that's the highlanders... We are an intelligent breed who doesn't believe anything anyone says until we can empirically prove it ourselves. Yes, this is what I meant. So I planted seeds and moved on.

John and I eventually went our separate ways and I put up my acrylic brushes and piano and tried my hand at soap making. It was around this time that I met my third wife.

An uphill climb in a downhill world

Sometimes life is so haphazard, so disruptive, so annoying and it seems like everything is passing by so quickly, and so furiously, that we forget what we are living for. It seems that all the beauty is lost in a sunset, or the fragrance of a flower is gone when we climb the ladder of life. Are we climbing too fast? Should we slow down? I say no. Who said life was a ladder anyhow? We are on the road of life, not the ladder. It is only through climbing the steep path that we can reach God. Not by trying to attain him as they did at the tower of Babel. Yes, I can see their pyramids of power, and their skyscrapers of success. But the story never changes. They are either traveling down the road, trying to build upwards by themselves, or they are wasting away at the side. I see very few who are going up with me. But I know I must go on. We must go on. we should travel together, you know. We should be able to trust in one another to be traveling companions. Can't we do that? Or, can we trust each other yet?

The road of life can be arduous, and seemingly meaningless at times, but we must know that God is on our side. Things go on around us everyday, and yet, we must be more than overcomers. We must rise above each occasion with the power of the triumphant one. Because greater is he that is in us than he that is in the world. Things happen to everyone. Both good and bad. Hey, it rains on the virtuous and the evil just the same. So why do we accept some of these things as from our Father? Don't get me wrong, I believe in Fire baptism, and I know that he chastises and rebukes those that he loves, but if I'm in a car wreak... I am not going to thank God (the giver of all good things) for it! I will not let those things happen to me! It is the thief that comes to kill steal and destroy, not the goodman of the house!

The only way that the thief can come in is if he first binds up the strong man. And then that violent one will take it by force, and by all means necessary, if possible. So, loose God, and let him do something for you! He is the "Abba" the da-da of all creation. Shall not the Father give his children good things if we ask it of him? Or who among you would give your kid a rock if he asks for some food? I shall stand firm on my belief that God actually likes and loves me. For it is not just a strong opinion, it is a solid fact.

Let your life be fun. Life was not intended to be a living Hell. It was intended for us to have fellowship with the creator, and to dominate creation. I shall walk the path no matter what happens! For He is still on my side. And when life seems to be crashing down around me, then I can still know that Jesus paid for it all. My salvation from Hell, accidents, and stress. And he sent his precious Holy Spirit to display the fact of his love. As a person in love with him, I would just like to say that he is my all in all. He is the one who tickles my fancy as well as my funny bone. I like him and He likes me. And he is proud when I can stand firm in the face of adversity, and having done everything that I know to do, stand in confidence.

What I usually do...

As I was pondering on how to best write these days, I thought of several different ways that would seem appropriate. As you might have guessed from other works of mine, I hold true to many tenants of Christianity. I also hold true to the fact that faith is a personal thing... not to be sold or bought cheaply without thinking. I never have thought of the most popular topics to write on, and I do not feel that I will win any awards for my ramblings. However, they are important to me... and for me to not write would be a sin.

As we humans are raised up into this world, we bring certain idealisms into our thought-collective. We see a glimmer of hope in a certain paradigm and thus swallow it up. Not bothering to seek a different way, but accepting the way given to us. Part of the foundation of Spiritual Christianity is to NOT accept those thoughts one has always had. Christianity is a challenge to those ideals and is always in contention within our hearts and our minds for supremacy. I have always asserted myself forward under these notions: I will reject my opinion and press on for TRUTH. This is one of my greatest challenges to this day.

The statement goes like this: Truth is only that which truth confirms. The concept of this is staggering.

But however true one corner of the jigsaw puzzle is... it is the complete opposite of the corner furthest from it. Like I am fond of saying: "A smart man learns from his own mistakes, but a wise man learns from the mistakes of others." I know that my truth is not your truth... but a part of the whole puzzle. Therefore I will surpass supposition.

However true experiences are, they can never rival the Word of God. And, so when in question; yours, mine, and all other Christians judgement falls under the authority of Jesus and the Holy Words of God.

I would say that it does not matter where your piece of the puzzle lays. True Spiritual Jesus-Loving is the focus of the "Pure". And as to that: the pure are the ones interested in building bridges from puzzle to puzzle... not tearing them down.